I'm a Truck

By Dennis Shealy
Illustrated by Bob Staake

In memory of my father, "Big Don" —DS

 A GOLDEN BOOK • NEW YORK

Library of Congress Control Number: 2004099569
ISBN: 0-375-83263-7
Printed in the United States of America
First Edition 2006
20 19 18

HOW-DEE!

My name's Big Blue Bill,
and I'm a truck. I've got
eighteen wheels turning,
six hundred horses under
the hood, and fifty-three
feet o' trailer hanging
on behind.

If there's a stretch of asphalt between Big Tuna and the Big Apple, I've ridden, rocked, bucked, and bounced down it, carrying one heavy load or another.

ICE CREAM
METROPOLIS
It's so yummy!
HOTEL
ROUTE 6A
STATE
55
ROUTE
CAUTION:
LOW CLEARANCE
IN TUNNEL
ONE WAY

Now, the highway is a big place to call home. On country roads, I see tractors tilling the soil and pulling special contraptions that plant seeds. Come harvest time, huge combines cut and pluck and gather up all the good food you eat.

VALLEY GRAIN CO.

Then pickups, flatbeds, and big trucks like me haul it to market.

Speaking of food, my fuel gauge is saying, "Big Blue Bill, you are *hun-greee.*" When that happens, there's no place like my favorite truck stop, where I refuel and *reee*-lax.

Hey, there's Polar Bear Pierre. He's refrigerated to keep milk and meat cold. Tanker Tina hauls gas and oil. And ol' Leif is a logging truck.

I may be the biggest truck on the road, but I'm not the only one. I can be halfway between nowhere and somewhere when along comes Bony Tony. He's a trailer truck that carries cars and small trucks to dealerships near you.

Good golly, there's Mo the tow truck. Looks
like my buddy Earl's down on his luck.
"How are ya feeling, Earl?"
"I've been better, Bill, but I'll be all right."

Detour?

Well, with all these cars and trucks on the road, sometimes you just have to make more road. Meet some of my biggest buddies.

Brunhilda the bulldozer comes through first, to clear the way. When she's finished pushing and shoving all that dirt, she calls her buddy Dirk the dump truck over to haul the rubble away.

Carl the grader comes along
next with his wide metal blade to
carve out the shape of the road.
"Hey, Carl! Ya missed a spot."

DETOUR

Dirty Al lays the asphalt—and *ooo-wee*, that asphalt is hot, stinky, and sticky till it cools. Lazy Al is a heavy steamroller that rolls right along behind him real slow to make the asphalt smooth as mashed potatoes. No lumps. No bumps.

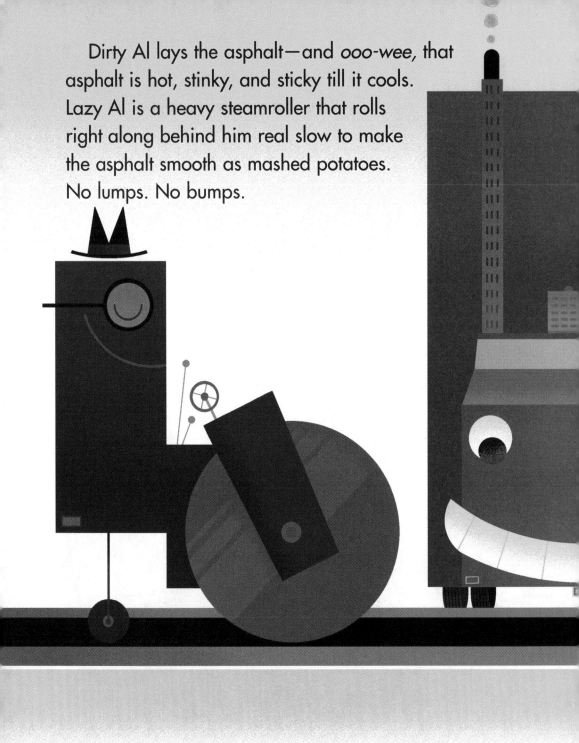

"Hey, boys, give me a lane, and make it double wide."

If you want to see
trucks bumper to bumper,
the city's the place to go.
But the last place I want to
be is stuck behind a garbage
truck. *Ooo-wee*, they make
Dirty Al seem downright rosy!

ROBOT TOY STORE

pizza

way at City Ave.

No matter what, I get out of the way fast when I hear a siren. Fire trucks, police cars, and ambulances have the most important job a vehicle can have— keeping you safe!

Firefighters put out fires with their big pumper trucks and rescue people from tall buildings with their ladder trucks. Police officers direct traffic safely out of the way. And if you get injured, you can just bet an ambulance will get you to the hospital mighty quick!

I love skyscrapers because my best buddies build 'em. Tipper drives around all day mixing cement. And Shorty, who's actually quite tall, lifts heavy steel beams so far into the air, my wheels get wobbly just thinking about it.

Pickups, bulldozers, backhoes, and more all work together to build buildings so tall, you'd think you could grab a piece of blue sky.

Well, here we are—the docks. It's time to drop off my load! Forklifts and cranes will put my freight on a cargo ship, and then it's off to parts unknown.

"Y'all be careful with that, now!"

As soon as I'm unloaded, I get reloaded, and then I'm off again. Those ships have an exciting life on the high seas . . .

. . . but I'm a truck and my home is the highway, so I'd best be getting down it. It's been real nice driving with ya, partner. Next time you see a truck, you tell 'im Big Blue Bill said

HOW·DEEE!